The Blonde Goddess of Tikka-Tikka

Tales of the Tomahawk - Volume I

Chris L. Adams

A Bizarre Tales© Publication

The Blonde Goddess of Tikka-Tikka

Copyright

The Blonde Goddess of Tikka-Tikka

Introduction

Several years ago, I got this idea for a tale which was to be influenced by the likes of H. P. Lovecraft—where the frail senses of humanity are called upon to confront nameless entities from other spheres of existence—and Robert E. Howard, who was as adept in his exploration of the Cthulhu mythos as he was in his creation of the Hyborian Age.

I always appreciated the way Howard's characters, when faced with something blasphemous "from beyond", rather than running away in fear with their sanity blasted they would instead fill their fists with cold steel and start slashing. Now, there is certainly something to be said for the manner in which Lovecraft handled the unnamable—that building of dread of which the Man who was Providence was a noted master. But burying an ax in a forehead comes with equal endorsement.

When I was still working on the amorphous ideas that eventually became *The Blonde Goddess of Tikka-Tikka* I asked a good friend for help in coming up with an interesting hero; we put our heads together, and I think the guy we created is perfect for this tale.

I hope you enjoy this short-story introduction to Ansen, a Norseman who was raised by an Arapaho medicine man.

Chris

Contents

Chapter 01: In the Jungle

Bezilbora, his eyes fixed unflinchingly on the object of his intent focus, walked quietly along a tree limb fifty feet above the matted growth surrounding the base of an immense acacia. Above him, in graceful loops, drooped many flowering lianas; these the savage swept silently from his path as he advanced along the broad limb of the jungle giant.

Bezilbora's naked feet gave forth no sound as he descended to a lower branch and crossed into another tree, every step made as silently as a ghost and with scarcely any disturbance of a single leaf. The group of individuals upon the ground remained completely oblivious of his presence.

In his mind, Bezilbora fantasized as to how Megrodomigran, the chief, might reward him for this creature. She was perfect for Koyltentapharr!

The young woman to whose allure Bezilbora had succumbed would draw the fascinated stares of the most sophisticated ladies' man of any civilized setting she graced with her presence, while her splendor would easily overcast a ballroom full of beauties. It is little wonder, then, that this untutored savage, having seen the girl, determined to capture her.

In a broad clearing below him—where decades ago a Goliath of the jungle had been struck by flashes of fire from the sky and had fallen, leaving the great dearth of growth but for the lush grasses growing in profusion around its corpse—a group of foreigners were pitching camp.

Porters hauled tents erect and staked them into place; *askarii*, toting rifles slung over glistening, ebon backs, erected a *boma* consisting of branches to circumscribe their camp site. For they well knew that great cats were wont to prowl at night, seeking their meals wherever they might find them.

But even more than predators of flesh and bone, they feared the woods of these islands to be supernaturally haunted. Already, many had sensed eyes upon them…

One member of the party took no part in these activities. He was a giant of a man, standing apart at the edge of the glowing circle of light cast by a nearby campfire with his enormous back to the flames, the Arapaho way when a man found himself in a strange country, far from home.

"A wise warrior will stare into the dark and keep the light of his fire behind him," old Tahnaktaka used to tell him as a boy. "By looking away from the flames, Owejiwa, your eyes remain in harmony with the darkness—a necessity if you wish to survive in the wilds…"

Especially if those wilds were the deep, foreboding jungle of an unknown island filled with stalking predators and night haunts.

"You're certainly a different sort there, Grost."

Cecil Sennet stopped beside the giant.

Not by the blink of an eye, the twitch of a muscle, or an audible sigh did the man standing at the edge of the firelight betray his aggravation at the other's unwanted attention.

Cecil was a Hollywood movie producer, a dandy, and was the reason the giant was standing in this jungle instead of sitting in that bar in Zimbabwe. Instinctively distrusting those who hailed from the world's cities, it had not been until their ship set sail that Cecil let it be known just what a milksop he was—a type for which one might seek, but never find, an ounce of respect.

"How do you figure?" he rejoined softly.

This giant of a man, Ansen Grost, looked like no Arapaho anyone ever laid eyes on because he was not native born of them, although he had been raised by them. But it was not the Arapaho, but rather a band of Shoshone that discovered a toddler Ansen in a wagon somewhere in the Utah wilderness.

"Well, for one, you are the only European I ever met who was raised by natives." Cecil barked a laugh then, "But, you're certainly not the first drunk Indian I ever met!"

Ansen's jaw clenched. He regretted letting the details of his upbringing slip when Cecil questioned him about the beads in his hair; but it was true, he'd been drunk at the time.

"I don't recall now, though, how you came to live with the Indians?" Cecil pressed.

"They're Arapaho. You were in your own cups that night," Ansen reminded the man tightly. "I don't recall that I elaborated."

It was years before Ansen knew even a portion of the answer to that question. His mother had left behind a diary which came to Tahnaktaka together with a bag of beads when the old shaman traded for the boy. The medicine man taught Ansen to read and write English without ever explaining how he himself had learned it. And although the diary was mostly in Norse, Ansen, with help from Tahnaktaka, puzzled out the few words for which his mother had adopted the English spelling.

"It seems your parents were headed west, from Pennsylvania, when they were attacked," Tahnaktaka mused, flipping the last few pages of the leather-covered diary. "Old Stone Crow told me the Shoshone launched the attack to avenge a decades-old wrong at the hands of the white-eyes. You were about three at the time,

Owejiwa. You were traded to various tribes until you came to dwell with the Arapaho."

A mane of golden hair fell past Ansen's massive shoulders, proclaiming the Nordic heritage bequeathed him by his Norwegian parents who migrated to the New World before he was born; his long locks were tied back with a leather wrap set with red beads. Bronzed skin stood in stark contrast with blonde locks; the features of his face were sharply angular and crowned with stormy gray eyes of inscrutable focus and clarity.

Cecil lit a cigarette and eyed Ansen in the aloof manner that some city folk reserve for those reared in the country. Changing the topic, he said, "That's quite some armament you carry around with you, Grost."

The shotgun Ansen cradled across his chest in arms the size of saplings was the same Winchester with which he slogged through the smoldering, corpse-riddled battlefields of France and Belgium. The Colt's automatic that swung from his angular hip had also been useful in clearing trenches in those days upon which he cared little to dwell.

For the most part Ansen's clothing and other impedimenta reflected the times of his day and age, the one exception being an ancient looking tomahawk thrust through the belt encircling his lean waist. The piece looked as if it might be hundreds of years old, bearing as it did the scars and marks of hard use.

"I stayed on in Europe after the war. I took these with me," Ansen explained. He gestured with the Winchester, "We used to call this a Trench Broom."

But Cecil was eyeing the tomahawk in Ansen's belt, his expression odd, as if the sight of it struck an ill note within him. "I never cared for such things," he said, taking a drag off his cigarette and quickly blowing the smoke into the humid night.

The ax's haft looked like it had been handled by the medicine men of a thousand generations, while the blade, honed and sharpened countless times during its untold days on the Earth, presented the chips and wear marks that come from the hard hammering of wood and bone.

"At the end of the day it's just a tool, Cecil, like any other," Ansen replied testily. "It gets the job done."

Cecil didn't reply; he only continued to stare.

The Blonde Goddess of Tikka-Tikka

Chapter 02: Abducted

When Grost hired-on with this expedition in Zanzibar as head of security, the job description intrigued him, being a position with a movie outfit out of Hollywood; and the proffered pay was phenomenal, which didn't hurt. A desperate Cecil explained that Ansen would be standing in for an extra who had not shown up for the shoot, and that the proffered salary was a reflection of the double-duty asked of him, insisting that Ansen was perfect for the part.

"I'm curious, Grost, what it was that persuaded you to take the job?" Cecil asked next, diverting his eyes from the tomahawk and taking another draw on his coffin nail. He looked at Ansen, "Was it the bonus?"

Ansen thought about it a moment before answering. It was something he learned from Tahnaktaka—don't be too quick to answer a question before giving it some thought.

"I needed the money, sure. But it wasn't just for the pay," he replied after a minute.

"Fame then?" pressed Cecil.

The Norseman didn't hesitate this time, "It wasn't for fame at all. Mostly, it was that you were traveling someplace no one ever heard of."

The Blonde Goddess of Tikka-Tikka

"That's right! You didn't seem interested in leaving your bar stool until I mentioned this uncharted island."

How these elite snobs from Hollywood learned of this island Ansen didn't know; but it offered him a chance to make a fistful of dollars and find a few weeks of forgetfulness for a melancholy wanderer from the plains of the American Midwest.

Thinking of the shores of this unknown chain of islands upon which they'd landed only that afternoon reminded him of his youth when he first began to stray off the lands of his people. Something within him had always driven him to explore beyond the tribal hunting grounds and his childhood haunts.

"Where are you going this time, Owejiwa?" the ancient medicine always asked him.

"If I knew that, there would be no need to go, would there?" Ansen would say.

Always in his youth had the horizon ever been his goal. Amongst the braves it was always Owejiwa who scouted the furthest afield, and Owejiwa who brought in the first kill from the approaching herds. Over time, the son of Tahnaktaka wandered further and further afield, staying away longer than he had in his youth. Sometimes absent for entire seasons, his stays with the tribe grew shorter, and the medicine man knew that one day his boy would leave and not return.

Ansen's reveries were abruptly interrupted from the area of the tents . . . a voice was shouting in alarm. Spinning, he saw the *askarii* with rifles leveled at a bizarre sight. In the dancing light of the cook fires stood a frightening apparition.

A giant native, naked but for a loin cloth, had dropped within their *boma* from the branches of a tree. Equipped with an enormous frame, the savage's heavily muscled body looked to have been developed from a lifetime spent in grueling effort—effort that taxed the man's muscles in ways they were not designed to be used.

The native's face was grotesquely painted to resemble a blue skull, his black eyes, surrounded as they were by black smudges, appearing like empty sockets. Skin piercings covered his body, with silver and golden ringlets running down his forearms, through his ears and his septum. Long, black hair, sprouting thickly from a low hairline, hung half-way down his back; upon one hip depended a foot-long knife.

To Ansen, the most daunting aspect of the man's appearance was the fact that he held Eva, the movie star, in his massive arms, the body of the woman substituting for armor in that it protected the savage from a hail of bullets from the *askarii* who dared not fire for fear of hitting her. Ansen only noticed these things in passing as he charged like a lion through the deep grasses covering their campsite in the direction of the savage crouching at the foot of the tree.

"*Tu sakka nu!*" the painted man shouted. "*Su attal— Koyltentapharr!*"

Before any could prevent it, the stranger dragged the girl behind the tree. They heard a slight disturbance in the foliage followed by a scream. An immediate hush fell upon the camp— but only for an instant.

For with the disappearance of the girl and the savage, the wails of the superstitious porters began. Wamibi, the headman, shouted orders to his *askarii* who immediately gutted a section of the *boma* they had just completed and began fanning out into the jungle in search of the abductor.

Ansen hit the tree at a run and charged up the bole like a squirrel. Entering the lower limbs, he climbed about, searching futilely for the girl, calling her name but receiving no response. She and her captor were gone. He dropped to the ground beside Wamibi. The entire episode had taken only seconds and had occurred across the encampment from him. Wamibi had been closer when the savage grabbed Eva, so it was from him he hoped to get any details the headman might have seen.

"Wamibi!" he asked the native. "Did you understand any of his strange talk?"

"No, *bwana*," replied the native, shaking his head negatively. "No boys I know talk like that!"

This small island chain lay some distance from the coast, out of the known paths of shipping lanes and the international flights of the new-fangled *zeppelins* and twin-propped aeroplanes. Who knew who settled here in the past? The strange language could belong to any race on the planet.

Cecil rushed up to the two, his eyes twin pools of fright. "What are you going to do—just stand there?" he screamed. "That man just kidnapped Eva!"

Ansen's eyes were smoldering with the desire to plant a heavy-knuckled fist in Cecil's face. Recalling that this was the man who hired him, he filed the idea away for possible later use.

"Yes, Cecil, I am aware of that," he replied coolly.

The hour waxed late, and they were all tired from the day's hike. And they had yet to prepare the evening meal, so they were all starving. But none of that mattered to Ansen as he began barking orders to his *askarii*. Shouldering packs of ammunition and rations, they prepared to enter the jungle in pursuit.

The few porters and *askarii* who had fanned into the forest to search for Eva were returning empty handed.

"It too dark," they muttered.

Ansen cursed. Through his mind flashed memories of hunting wolf, cougar and bear through trackless wastes and lightless nights in the wilds of America. Gripping a lantern in one rough hand and his shotgun in the other, he barked his orders, and set out, with fifteen armed men at his back.

Chapter 03: Pursuit

Ansen was surprised when the producer fell-in behind the armed men as they tromped into the nighted jungle. He accounted himself a good judge of character and had pegged the man from Hollywood for an errant coward and a pantywaist. He wouldn't expect to find any more backbone in Cecil than a scientist might discover upon dissecting an invertebrate. He was glad the man accompanied them, however, as they needed every eye scouring the forest for sign of the kidnapper.

Naturally, there could be no way of knowing which direction the abductor had taken the girl. After walking fifty yards, Ansen called a halt. Slinging his shotgun over his shoulder he clambered into the branches of a jungle giant, using the yellowish light of his lantern to look for clues, limiting his search amongst branches sturdy enough to support simultaneously the kidnapper and his prey.

In this manner he began circling and in about twenty minutes he found something. About twenty feet above the ground he noticed where a twig had snapped from the passage of a body. Nearby, the grinding pressure of a callused foot—a foot bearing more weight than normal—scuffed the bark; the girl's abductor was taking her northwest.

The Blonde Goddess of Tikka-Tikka

Dropping to earth, Ansen called to his men. "They went this way," he said. And signaling with his lantern which shined like a beacon in the nighttime forest, they set out on the trail of the savage whose face was painted like a blue skull.

They found their way hard fought as the jungle floor was matted with all manner of vegetation. Machetes in hand, they hacked and hewed their way forward. Cecil was silent, offering no complaint from the myriad stinging insects that swarmed them, a fact that Ansen found curious as the man tended to gripe at the slightest provocation.

A massive spider web, suspended between low hanging branches, caught Ansen square across the face as he forged a path, and an icky, bloated body turned to pulp under his palm when he swiped the mess away. But Ansen wasn't one to worry too much over hardships or inconveniences, not even the disgusting ones.

"At least it wasn't a giant banana spider," he muttered.

"Those are the worst," agreed Wamibi, grinning in the darkness at his boss's discomfiture. "You should have eaten it. We all are starving, and you pass on a meal like that!"

"Shuttup, Wamibi," Ansen grinned.

Occasionally he climbed into the trees to look for evidence that they were still on the trail of their quarry. Once, he nearly couldn't find a trace of them. It took him forty minutes of diligent searching before he discovered that their prey had come to ground on a well-worn trail a hundred yards to their west, a trail that Ansen's party was unknowingly paralleling.

He returned to the men and sought Wamibi.

"We must tread quietly," whispered Ansen. "There is a trail just over there. The natives will certainly watch it, perhaps signaling ahead to ambush us."

As quietly as possible given the darkness, the men slunk along, their lights extinguished now. Luckily, the jungle night was raucous and alive with sound. The cries of hunter and hunted frequently broke the stillness, along with mating calls and the buzzing of insects, all of which Ansen prayed would disguise any noise his troops made. Shortly, the trail exited the dark forest into a small clearing. Ansen paused.

"I don't know about this," he murmured to Wamibi. "Feels like a setup."

Wamibi nodded. "We should tread carefully, *bwana.*"

As they stood in the shadows discussing it, Cecil approached, forcing his way through the *askarii*. "What are we waiting for, Grost? Eva is in God knows what danger! We need to hurry."

"You should really keep your tactical opinions to yourself Cecil. I wouldn't dare advise you on how to shoot a scene, because I know nothing about it," Ansen retorted pointedly. Sighing, he turned to Wamibi. "He is right about one thing. Miss Desyre is depending on us. Keep your eyes peeled, all of you."

Ansen stepped into the clearing with his neck prickling. Cautiously, the men fell in behind him and started across.

Without warning, a sharp sting pierced Wamibi's neck, where he walked beside the great *bwana*. Smacking what he presumed to be another irritating insect the Zimbabwean was surprised to feel a firm body attached to him—a slender, rigid body with a fluffy end.

"A poison dart," he shouted. "*Bwana*! We are attacked!'

Already Wamibi felt a sluggishness spreading outwardly into his extremities; he staggered. Raising his rifle, the headman fired without aiming into the tree line across the clearing before sinking to the ground to speak no more; the fast-acting venom dropped him in seconds. In the flash of Wamibi's rifle a face appeared briefly.

The Blonde Goddess of Tikka-Tikka

"There!" an *askarii* cried, firing.

Ansen spun at the shout, surprised to note a lessening of the surrounding darkness; the moon was rising. And, although the orb had not yet climbed high enough that it could be seen, it yet cast a glow that filtered between the boles of the trees. In the trees he saw a smudge of misshapen darkness upon a large branch. P*hhhht*—the native who last spoke screamed and clutched his throat before dropping to the ground beside Wamibi.

"They're in the trees across the clearing!" Ansen cried, and then he fired a blast at the indistinct form with his shotgun. The shadowy shape dropped from the limb and disappeared amidst the darker obscurity of the riotous flora upon the matted floor of the primordial forest across from them.

The *askarii* fired at will, their muzzle flashes revealing faces and forms crouching in the trees surrounding them; they'd walked into a trap.

The garishly painted savages were equipped with spears and blow guns, the latter of which they made lavish use. Screams sounded on all sides as Ansen's men were shot to death by poisoned darts, their screams originating more from the psychological horror produced by the darts than the actual pain induced by the stinging pricks of the barbed deaths that flew at them out of the surrounding darkness, missiles they stood no chance to avoid.

Ansen realized they must take the battle to these fellows or they were done for. Slinging his shotgun over his shoulder he ran to the bole of a tree and started climbing, keeping the jungle giant between him and the attacking natives as best he might.

"Blast it," he muttered as he climbed. "Did we ever stumble into it!"

Chapter 04: Death in the Moonlight

Ansen guessed there were at least a hundred savages, based on the tell-tale glimpses he saw in the flashes of gunfire. The real numbers could be more, he realized.

A dark shape appeared in his path. Without pause, he stabbed his forty-five automatic at the face and squeezed the trigger. Advancing, Ansen came upon another form that he batted aside with the barrel of the gun, grunting in satisfaction at the scream of the falling warrior, and the sound of snapping branches as the body plummeted to the hard ground.

As sure-footed as the mountain lions he stalked in the hills as a boy, he ran out upon a gigantic limb he had selected from which to launch his attack. The length of it extended into a neighboring tree swarming with howling wild men. The numbers of Ansen's *askarii* who were still in the fight had dropped significantly, judging by the decrease in gunfire. He guessed there to be less than five or six of his men still standing.

"They're getting the best of us," he whispered hoarsely.

By the glint of moonlight upon faces painted like blue skulls, he dropped into the midst of three or four of the enemy before they were aware of his presence. No sooner had he alighted upon the branch than he pulled his shotgun from his back and unloaded a round directly in the face of the nearest savage. The man's face, and most of his head, disappeared, and the body spun backwards from the blast and dropped into the weeds and tangled brush below, taking the dead man's nearest companion with him in his flight from the branch.

Ansen was an old hand at this and so, with undimmed sight, he pivoted, automatically wracking the action to load another shell into the breach of his model '97. He stuck the shotgun into the belly of another painted warrior. The same moment he squeezed the trigger he snapped his eyes shut against the blinding flash, opening them an instant later to note the effect. The body, blown several feet out into space, described an arc toward the ground.

Satisfied, he advanced upon the next one. This warrior had been staring in Ansen's vicinity when the American fired his previous round. The brilliant fireball, coming as it did out of the darkness, caused the savage to see dancing stars in front of his eyes. Temporarily blinded, the savage lunged at him with a spear. Ansen batted the man's clumsy thrust aside with the shotgun's barrel, worked the action and squeezed the trigger—nothing happened. The weapon needed to be loaded but he had no time to do so.

To some these things would require conscious thought—to both realize one clutched an empty weapon and to automatically grab the choicest backup without hesitation. In the trenches of Europe, Ansen witnessed men in the heat of battle frantically squeezing the triggers of empty firearms, not comprehending that they needed to reload.

It was only later in life that the blonde giant had acquired firearms, but he practiced with them until his proficiency became notable amongst his peers. Prior to that, he'd mastered the knife, the bow, the spear—and the tomahawk. Many times, he had been in predicaments when only split-hair moments lie between his continuing to walk the Earth and his joining the spirit world. His reflexes by now were so instinctual that his reactions were as unconscious as breathing.

His shotgun rendered momentarily useless, the American immediately filled his fist, not with the forty-five slung low upon one lean hip which he'd brought to bear earlier and which, for many, would have been the natural selection, but instead with the tomahawk that had for years been his constant companion.

This weapon was old long before he'd been born and bore the scars of many battles. It had been handed down to Tahnaktaka from his father, who had in turn received it at his own coming of age. No man could gauge its years upon the Earth, yet its worth in war was obvious when one's fingers wrapped about its studded, sweat-stained haft.

In less than a second the ancient tomahawk feasted on fresh spilt blood and brains. Before, as he fought, Ansen had shouted encouragement to his *askarii*. He'd cursed as lustily as any other, his savage insults and Billingsgate blasting the ears of the enemy as he cursed them, their forebears and their progeny. The fact that they couldn't understand him made no difference.

But now it was not language, but the wordless howl of the Arapaho who has killed in war and the Viking warrior who faces his foe in armed conflict that filled the air—a cry so savage, so primal in its fierceness, and so visceral in its gloating over the fallen slain, that it caused near-instant, ripe fear to blossom in the hearts of all those who heard it.

It was at this moment that the Old Man in the Moon looked down in his full glory upon the scene. Silvery-white light bathed the bloody clearing in the forest where the natives sought to slaughter Ansen and his men. Only two of the *askarii* remained standing, one of them feverishly loading his weapon with a shaking hand. The other, even as he lifted his rifle, Ansen saw swat at a place upon his breast, glance down, and then pitch forward into the trampled grasses.

The remaining warrior, having finished loading his weapon, looked up in time to witness Ansen leap from his perch toward a point several feet below the Norseman. The white man's arms were drawn back, both his fists gripping the haft of some weapon he'd swung to a position far behind him. In that moment, his godlike flight caused him to look like some heroic and mythical figure.

Mesmerized by the dazzling sight, the *askarii* stood stock still, watching, until he felt a sting in his neck. He swatted at the spot almost absentmindedly. For the life of him, he could not tear his eyes from the figure of the Arapaho warrior.

As his knees buckled beneath him from the effects of the poisoned barb, he caught the glint of moonlight off the wicked edge of the ax in the *bwana's* hands. Ansen's body flew through the air and, timed to absolute perfection, the tomahawk swung viciously, describing an arc that ended its grim journey in the cranium of a warrior upon whom Ansen had focused his undivided attention.

And then the *askarii's* rifle fell from nerveless fingers, and, collapsing, he knew no more.

Chapter 05: Last Man Standing

Of Ansen's troupe he alone lived, his men lying scattered in lifeless heaps about the clearing. Blood drenched the forest floor about the edges of the glade from the ventilated bodies of the attackers that had fallen to his and the *askarii's* hails of gunfire.

Many of the ambushers weren't deceased, though, and these moaned in agony from non-fatal gunshot wounds and falls. Others of them sprawled haphazardly, blown nearly in half by Ansen's shotgun or shot through by the powerful European rifles with which Wamibi and the *askarii* were armed.

The surviving painted devils faced off now—not against modern rifles—but against a weapon that the colonials of the New World considered a holy terror in the times their wagon trains crossed the wilds of America back in the day as they sought to wrest lands from those whom they considered heathens.

With knife, bow and ax, *The People's* ancient progenitors fought the more heavily armed frontiersmen in olden times; but of all the weapons the natives brought to bear in defense of their homeland, the tomahawk had been as revered among *The People* as it had been feared amongst the Europeans. With this weapon, *The People* split the skulls of men and women alike. But today the ax in Ansen's fist severed limbs and blasted foreheads on an island whose existence remained unknown to the modern-day world.

The Blonde Goddess of Tikka-Tikka

Ansen never questioned how the movie producers, come to these parts to film "jungle scenes" for their film, learned of this savage place. But none of that mattered now. Ansen had lost sight of Cecil at the first onslaught. For all he knew the whining, pestilential coward was halfway to their campsite where he would likely hide behind his film crew. But the Norwegian had little time for thoughts of Cecil Sennet or any other, only to slay until he himself lay among the fallen slain.

Dragged from a tree limb by a native who clutched Ansen's ankle to save himself from falling, the American resumed his fight amidst the trampled grasses of the moonlit clearing. He hadn't found time to reload his shotgun, but it didn't matter as it was lost to him after it fell into the underbrush. He stood gripping his bloody tomahawk in one raw-knuckled fist, trying to recall how many shots he'd fired from his automatic, which only held seven rounds.

The howling natives, having circled Ansen, converged on him with leveled spears. He wondered briefly why they didn't shoot him with their blow guns and guessed they'd ran out of poison darts. They didn't immediately cast their stone-tipped weapons, though, causing him to wonder if they wanted to take him alive to torture him while others of their numbers assaulted the campsite to kill or capture the porters and film crew.

Seeing that they completely hemmed him, he realized that they could not cast their spears without risking hitting their own; Ansen took a firmer grip on his ax as they closed the circle more tightly. Before they could pierce him with their stone-tipped spears, an elaborately dressed man whom Ansen recognized as a shaman, advanced. He shouted at the natives, who then reversed their spears, with the blunt ends raised as bludgeons.

Ansen did the only thing remaining to him—he fought. It was the only part of the equation of which he had any control. The Arapaho warrior whirled and spun and slashed at the spear-swinging savages, his braids flying wildly, determined to take as many of them with him into the spirit world as possible.

"By the *Sky*!" he roared, sumping his ax into a tough and savage skull; it cracked like a nut.

The tomahawk, smeared in gore, killed and maimed with Ansen's every move. One side of the star-metal head was forged into a straight-edged blade spanning four inches. On the opposite side was a blunt, hammerhead used to deal crushing blows or drive tent pegs. The handle, a thick piece of mammoth ivory studded with brass studs for tactility, ended in a spike. Ansen knew from experience how quickly that spike could turn a healthy eye into an empty socket.

Ansen ripped the blade from the face in which he had buried it and slammed it back-handed into the face of a different savage, the hammer caving in the nose and upper palate and burying into the skull, killing the man instantly. The action of jerking the weapon free destroyed the remainder of the dead man's face, leaving the corpse looking like a human travesty as it fell amongst its fellows who simply ignored it as they trampled the body underfoot to get at Ansen.

In pure berserker frenzy Ansen fought, his long hair—wetted by contact with the blood of his enemies—flying outward in gory tendrils to his gyrations, clutching the short, brutal ax in two hands so that when it hacked into the neck of its next victim the body fell nearly beheaded. The pile of bodies surrounding the Norseman mounted, yet the savages kept coming, there seeming no limit to the numbers they were willing to sacrifice to capture him alive.

At any time could his attackers could have withdrawn and cast their spears at the ax-wielding Arapaho, but whenever one offered to thrust at him with the long blade of a spear, Megrodomigran, their chief, shouted threateningly, at which point the offending warrior would retreat and approach the blonde-haired barbarian with the blunt end of his weapon once more raised as a bludgeon.

This only continued for a few minutes before Megrodomigran cried out new instructions. The glistening bodies of his warriors—drenched in sweat and blood—withdrew at their chief's command. From encircling Ansen they now formed their numbers into the shape of a crescent moon, but still closely pressing the man that he might not flee into the forest. The instant they were in position, freshly fetched poison-tipped projectiles sped toward their target—the breast of Ansen Grost.

The Arapaho warrior felt the barbs pierce his body and recognized the sting of the poison as it coursed through his veins, his blood pumped forcefully by a heart hammering wildly after a half hour of vigorous, hand-to-hand fighting.

He had often wondered how he would face his death. Now that it was upon him, he was surprised that he felt exhausted, but was unafraid. His chest rose and fell as the warriors before him dimmed and split into blurry images of which he could no longer tell which were real and which were phantoms.

The savages withdrew out of reach of Ansen's tomahawk but that did not matter since the man no longer had the energy to wield his ax. But he did manage to haul his automatic from its leather holster. The weapon barked three times before it ran dry with the slide locked back.

Two savages fell to the ground to rise no more.

The Arapaho warrior stumbled to his knees.

The savages, chanting mumbo jumbo that sounded wild and rhythmic to Ansen's Westerner's ears, converged on him, the blunt ends of their spears raised. Nearly unconscious, Ansen resisted weakly as the first of many blows from the enraged islanders' spear hafts rained upon him—but he fell to ground unconscious and never knew it.

Chapter 06: Village of Stone

Dimly, Ansen Grost heard shouts and cries of torment and fear—the kind of fear that causes a grown man to blubber like a child. The sounds came muffled to his ears, so he could not understand them. He felt, in that moment, as if he floated, bodiless, without conscious thought or of awareness of form. But that did not last long.

Soon the voices began taking meaning in his muddled mind, as did the agony in his body where the savages had beat him. He had only survived the ordeal because Megrodomigran forced his warriors away from the American's unconscious form with the application of the ceremonial staff of his station, an implement fashioned from a single bone taken from some unknown creature and carved with spirals of miniature human skulls along its length. At its top was a large, jaw-less skull which was reddened now with the blood of his own subjects.

Opening his eyes, the Norseman looked upon a sight few had beheld—and none that had, had lived to speak of it. Surrounding him were his *askarii* with whom he had set out in search of the actress. Those whom he'd believed were dead he now learned were alive and penned in wooden cages such as that in which he lay. Everywhere were savages such as those they'd fought, all busily engaged in various tasks about the village; the night had passed, and it was now the next day.

The Blonde Goddess of Tikka-Tikka

Bare-breasted women with somewhat angular features like Ansen's own and with long, intricate braids hanging down their backs, processed the bodies of the slain—all of whom were their fellow tribesmen. These people had an affinity for adorning their muscular bodies with bracelets and piercings of precious metals, and the Norseman saw plenty of gold and platinum displayed in abundance upon these women—an abundance which the destitute wastrel in him eyed narrowly.

Everywhere children ran amok, occasionally chastised by a warrior or a female of the tribe. Great cauldrons steamed as chunks of meat, sliced from the corpses of those who had perished in the fighting, were tossed unceremoniously into the cook pots. Other corpses, having been field dressed and skinned, they smoked. Ansen guessed the smoke cured meat was destined for consumption later, while the boiled cuts would be enjoyed by the tribe directly.

But these things were not what at last riveted Ansen's attention. His eyes were soon drawn, not to the goings on of the tribe into whose hands he and his men had fallen, but to the massive cliffs at their backs. The rocky face towering into the air was covered with the facades of habitations, as evidenced by dark entries leading within. Up and down the face of the cliff were carved hand and foot holds that gave these people ingress to their domiciles.

Ansen watched a villager begin at the bottom, sling a load over a shoulder, and start up the precipitous cliff as if it were a simple footpath. The savages were prone to take shortcuts to their destinations by leaping for handholds or footholds lying beyond their reach with the confidence of a lifetime of clambering about on this vertical surface. Watching them explained the unusual muscular development of this savage people, although their origin must remain veiled in obscurity.

Sometimes a face would peer out of an opening, glance down to see if the path was clear, and then drop over the edge with the agility of a simian and descend to the ground in moments although the distance might be nearly the full height of the cliffs. Ansen watched two women, approaching on the same path, pass one another by the simple expedient of one crossing over the other with the surety of an insect crawling down a tree trunk.

Now Ansen looked further upward, to the top of the cliffs, where he saw yet another strange sight. Extending outward over the precipice were what appeared to be twenty or thirty crudely fashioned cranes manufactured of roughhewn timbers. From these contraptions long, braided ropes depended to the ground.

"What in the name of the *Sky*?" he wondered.

While Ansen observed these things, hulking warriors, their faces made hideous by the awful paint schemes they'd adopted—but possessing handsome features otherwise—approached one of the cages. It was Wamibi's cage before which they stopped, whom Ansen thanked *Father Sky* to see was still alive after he believed him dead.

The warriors shouldered wooden poles attached to the headman's cage, many of which appeared to have been but newly made as the wood was freshly hewn. Bending to their work, they began to carry Wamibi away.

"*Bwana!*" the headman cried out as they took hold of his cage and lifted it from the ground.

"Stop that! What are you doing?" Ansen shouted futilely at the backs of the mute warriors. "Stand fast, Wamibi!"

But where Ansen thought to see Wamibi carried to a cook pot they instead bore him to a position below which savages at the top of the cliffs now dropped a heavy, braided rope from one of the wooden structures upon the precipice. This rope the warriors upon the ground attached to Wamibi's cage and then those on the precipice began hauling the Zimbabwean upward. Soon, the frightened headman dangled high in the air with nothing more between him and the hard, rocky ground than thin air.

The Blonde Goddess of Tikka-Tikka

Wondering what was the point of all this, Ansen watched as the warriors once more approached the cages holding him and his men.

Chapter 07: Eva

"Ansen!"

Upon awakening, the Viking had been distracted by the sight of his men being hauled up the side of a cliff to *Father Sky* knew what end. Turning painfully at the sound of his name—for he had not come through the previous night unscathed—Ansen discovered the vibrant blonde cast to play the part of the goddess in a jungle movie destined to never be filmed looking at him; she was similarly caged.

The girl's brilliant blue eyes brimmed with tears, and her Cupid's bow lips were drawn in a worried pout. "Ansen Grost!" the distraught girl cried out again. "I feared you were dead!"

"Miss Desyre!" he replied. "I'm fine. But you, were you harmed?"

"Please, call me Eva. No, I wasn't harmed. I must have fainted as that terrifying man carried me through the trees. We were so high!"

"I'm sorry," he replied.

"I would have screamed, but my voice caught in my throat. When I awoke, I was lying in this cage," she finished.

Taking in her disheveled form, Ansen recalled the moment in the pub in Zanzibar where he was mulling the producer's offer over a couple of whiskeys when this very woman glided through the door and approached the bar where he had sat. She walked straight up to an empty barstool beside him and sat down, although there were empty tables and spots at the bar where she might have sat alone, had she chosen. Every eye in the room followed her every curvaceous step.

"Well?" she asked as she sat, crossing one leg over the other.

The action revealed creamy slices of flesh nearly to her waist and Ansen became at once the envy of every grifter, thief, vagabond, and workhand in the pub. He swallowed the burning, amber fluid in his tumbler and plunked the empty glass down on the bar.

"Well . . . what?" he asked.

"Are you going to take the job? I'm Eva Desyre by the way," she introduced herself, "the star of the picture. I should think you would enjoy the role," she encouraged. "The character is very much like your real self, as Cecil described you. You play an intrepid explorer, battling your way across an African jungle in search of a fabled city of gold. You know—Tarzan stuff."

The girl eyed him up and down, admiring his physique. "I see now why Cecil recommended you. You would have no problem landing a role as a Tarzan."

"What's the name of the movie?" he asked. "Sennett, never said."

"The Blonde Goddess of Tikka-Tikka," she replied.

"Interesting," he replied noncommittally. "And what role will you be playing?"

Eva smiled until he grinned in return.

Squatting in her cage, Eva closed her eyes as if reliving the journey of horror where Bezilbora carried her through a pitch-black forest. Ansen imagined how it must have been for a socialite such as she—the proverbial maiden tossed over the withers of her captor's horse, so to speak—to be carried away by force like the spoils of conquest to an unknown fate.

"Do you have any idea what their intentions are?" he asked. He knew they needed to come up with a plan of escape, and quickly. He examined more closely the structure in which they were imprisoned. The branches were thick, tough and green. The braided rope seemed impregnable sans the presence of a knife or other sharp implement.

At that thought, his hand shot to his belt.

The tomahawk! Owejiwa was gone!

Chapter 08: *Owejiwa*, the Ax

"No!" he burst. "I've lost *Owejiwa!*"

Ansen was given his Arapaho name, Owejiwa, by *The People* when they adopted him into the tribe—the name selected by the medicine man who raised him. Per custom, the tomahawk, a talisman of the tribe, assumed the name of its bearer the day fate decreed that he inherit the ancient token of power. At one time the talisman was known as *Tahnaktaka*, foreswearing the name of its previous conveyor when the medicine man was chosen to carry it.

"What?" asked Eva, confused. "What is an *Owejiwa?*"

"My tomahawk," Ansen whispered.

"You mean that hatchet you've been carrying around with you since we boarded ship in Zanzibar?"

To *The People*, the tomahawk and Owejiwa were spiritually adjoined. *Owejiwa* —no mere hatchet—was a talisman of great power, and Owejiwa the man was the bearer of the mighty token; they were one and the same. Ansen had carried and kept it safe for years. It had protected and supported the tribe, it had slain by his hand leopard, bear, wolf, and man . . . and things not of mankind.

"It's not a hatchet," he replied absently, looking about on the ground, knowing he wouldn't find it there.

The Blonde Goddess of Tikka-Tikka

The conversation he had with Tahnaktaka the day he inherited the ax came back to him. Ansen crouched low to enter the sweat lodge, being a head taller than the men of his tribe. Tahnaktaka, the most revered medicine man of all the tribes of the Arapaho nation, had been in the lodge for three days without emerging. When Ansen returned that morning from the hunt he received word that his father awaited him.

As he entered the hot, confined space, the pungent effluvium of smoke and sweat assailed his nostrils. Beads of water sprouted upon his brow and rolled in rivulets down his back. The old man bade him sit across from him upon the other side of the pit of glowing coals. Without preamble, Tahnaktaka passed his adopted son a well-worn pipe filled with the aromatic blending of strange herbs. While Ansen puffed it to life, Tahnaktaka spoke, the drifting tendrils causing the old man's face to appear as a mirage drifting over the fire beds of Hell.

"Soon you will sail over the great water," Tahnaktaka announced abruptly.

Ansen nearly choked on his pipe smoke. He had told no one of his plans to leave the tribe and head west. Since his youth he had dreamed of the ocean. His father's stories of the voyage at sea that brought his family to America's shores were forgotten by him yet must have left an impression on the toddler; his parents' people were a seafaring people. He could barely remember them, and was only able to conjure vague images, but he recalled that his mother was lovely and kind.

The old man let out a throaty laugh at the startled expression on Ansen's face and then reached down beside him and passed the younger man the tomahawk of ancient and curious make. Ansen had seen this weapon many times when Tahnaktaka brought it out for sacred rituals, and dire needs.

Once, decades before Ansen came to dwell with him, a chief came from a more easterly tribe and begged Tahnaktaka to use it in revenge against the horse soldiers of the white man. Tahnaktaka refused. It was a token, the medicine man explained, of power and could not be used basely. The tomahawk was a defender of the tribe—but more than that, it was a defender of humanity against the tide of supernatural powers that would enslave mankind, if given the opportunity.

"But . . . Tahnaktaka! I cannot take this!" Ansen had exclaimed.

"Father Sky protects his people. *He* says you will need it," Tahnaktaka replied in a tone that brooked no argument.

Ansen was a stubborn boy in his youth, one who at all times was unwilling to follow the dictates of authority or allow others to direct his destiny.

"But . . . I am not of *The People*," he denied, starting at the proffered talisman.

"Owejiwa, the time has come that you must bear this burden—not I. I alone shall now bear the name to which I was born—Tahnaktaka. From this day forth, the talisman's true name shall be—*Owejiwa!*" the medicine man proclaimed.

Seeing that it was useless to argue, the youth acquiesced with a terse nod. Tentatively, Ansen extended his hands into which the wise, old man placed the scarred haft of the ancient weapon that stood as a sigil against darkness, a destroyer of wickedness and a standard bearer for humanity.

"You have filled the cook pots of the widows and orphans, Owejiwa. You have stood with the tribe against its enemies. You *are* of *The People*," Tahnaktaka finished with finality.

The medicine man's tone was such that it caused a young Ansen to bite his tongue against any arguments he might have made.

Chapter 09: Atop the Cliffs

Ansen's thoughts came back to the present, where he lay imprisoned in a wooden cage on an unknown island off the coast of Africa, not sitting in a medicine lodge among the tents of *The People*.

"How might the token be of any use if I no longer possess it," he muttered. "How will it combat evil if it falls into the hands of evil-doers? What would you do, Tahnaktaka?"

He looked to the girl; she was staring at him—it was an odd stare which he found confusing, given their circumstances, and from which he could fathom nothing. But he knew she was depending on him to save her—all of them were.

One after the other, the natives carried his men to the base of the cliff and hauled them upward. Already, a dozen men dangled in their cages, suspended over a stupendous fall should the wooden structures collapse, or a hand-braided rope suddenly snap under the pressure of the swinging cage it held aloft. Ansen had yet to make the journey—he and the girl were still awaiting their turns, wondering what their ultimate disposition was to be once they reached the top of the cliffs.

While they awaited their fates a war party exited the forest into the clearing with the porters and the camera crew in tow. These were tied by the neck and daisy-chained together to prevent flight. The faces of the porters were long, and the whites of their eyes showed plainly in their fright. The camera crew—all city slickers from California—looked dazed, as if they could not quite believe what was happening.

This wasn't the first time Ansen had found himself in such straits. During the Great War, the Germans captured him out in No Man's Land, and announced that he was to be shot at dawn. That night he chewed through his bonds, killed his guards along with the captain who had condemned him to death, and snuck back to his own lines, arriving in time for breakfast. With him he had a map case full of important documents and the Prussian officer's Luger stuck in his belt.

But this time there wouldn't be any chewing through his bonds. He watched as the new arrivals were caged, with one of the cinematographers being carried at once to the foot of the cliffs. The man screeched in fear. Ansen shook his head; city folk did not know how to control their fear or face their final moments in peace and tranquility, with honor and integrity.

"They are not of *The People*," he said to himself, the smile on his face a grim one.

Eva was watching Ansen's profile at the time and noticed the smile on his Scandinavian features, although she hadn't caught his words.

"Your bravery is not something you put on like a smoking jacket, Ansen Grost. I saw you just now. You literally smile in the face of death! Bravery like that cannot be feigned," she stated flatly, admiration in her tone.

"I will die, if that is the wish of *Father Sky*," he replied. "But I'm not unafraid! Only a fool has no fear. But I don't have to let it control me. When the time comes, I will fight like a panther and die as befits an Arapaho warrior."

Ansen knew he would most likely die trying to escape whatever fate these savages had in store for him. But he was of the stuff that would fight until his heart ceased to beat, and only bided his time for the opportunity. He would sense when the moment had ripened, and he would strike.

"They are coming for us, now," the girl said calmly, watching over Ansen's shoulder the approach of the natives assigned to carry the prisoners to the foot of the cliff.

Looking, he saw that she was right.

Ansen's turn had come. Brawny warriors stooped before his cage and bent their backs to the burden of his weight combined with that of his cage, grunting as they did so. He found himself jostled as they made their way across the precarious, rocky terrain to the foot of the stone face where they then tied a braided rope to a point at the top of his cage.

Soon he was making the dizzying trip, his cage swinging pendulously as they hauled him upward with the cliff face some eight- or ten-feet distance from him. After several minutes he had been raised above the level of the precipice.

The vantage point offered magnificent views of miles of jungle verdure. Rivers snaked through the forest, steam rising from their surface as they reached sea level elevations from mountainous heights at the center of the island from which they sprang. The ship that brought them here was barely visible in the distance, making him wonder if he had noticed these cliffs while still aboard; he couldn't recall.

The heights offered Ansen, who was unafraid of falls, little to fear. He spent the time watching as they brought the girl's cage to a position adjacent to that from which his own cage had left the ground. Before he reached a point a quarter of the way up, the savages began hauling the girl upward, and so she arrived shortly after he.

Evening was coming on. The sun, a bloody red disk in the sky, dyed the cumulonimbus in bright shades of pink and lavender as it dipped into a watery horizon. Visible along the cliff in the reddish glow of the sunset were the hanging cages filled with porters, *askarii*, the camera crew and the rest—Eva, Cecil, and Ansen.

It was the first Ansen had seen of the movie producer since the previous evening. But beyond that, it was perhaps, the most peculiarly weird and deadly scene he had ever witnessed.

The Norseman began to tense.

"This is it," he said. "Whatever they're going to do, they're going to do it now."

Chapter 10: Tortment

As Ansen watched, the villagers who were still on the ground swarmed up the face of the cliff. The children, the women, the warriors—one and all scurried towards the cliff-top as if they sought to escape an approaching flood.

As they topped the cliff the villagers stepped quickly away from the edge, as though fearful. Ansen knew they did not fear the vertiginous heights upon which he had watched them clamber fearlessly, and so wondered what it was that frightened them.

Megrodomigran, their chief, stepped to a podium of sorts, a raised dais made of stone with a slab in the center that grimly resembled the altars Ansen had seen at the ruins of Cholula and Kalibangān during his wanderings.

They pivoted the first in the line of dangling cages around on its wooden mechanism, lowered it to the stone, and dragged a man forth—he was one of the porters. The Viking winced.

"And so it begins," he muttered fiercely.

"What begins,?" Eva asked.

The terrified man's eyes rolled in fright; the whites of his eyes standing in stark contrast against his ebon face. He would have been screaming hideously, the Viking knew, had they not stuffed his mouth with the skin of some animal, the wad then bound in place with sinew behind the man's head. Roughly, they threw him across the altar and bound him fast to the surface and then the warriors withdrew once more to a point next to the cages.

Four others, acolytes of the chief, took positions at each corner of the altar while the chief stood at a position at the porter's head.

In a sing-song chant, Megrodomigran began reciting a ritual that was ancient when Ansen's Arapaho forebears crossed the land bridge thousands of years before to propagate their races in the Americas. Torches, protruding from holes in the stone, arranged in strange but obvious patterns about the surface of the cliff, cast their garish illumination upon the doomed man's glistening skin—skin drenched with the stinking sweat of a hideous fear.

Ansen never saw a signal but, as if on cue, the four men at the corners began pummeling the bound man's limbs with heavy mallets, beginning at the extremities. At each concussion of the blunt instruments the man's bones were shattered, and in this manner, they worked their way towards his torso until his arms and legs resembled split, bleeding shapeless sacks of broken pottery. Ansen, although sickened by the sight, could not tear his eyes from the worse torment he ever witnessed a human being suffer.

At some point he realized that even through the stuffed animal skin in the man's mouth he discerned a high pitched, ringing squeal, and somehow comprehended that it issued from the porter's throat. Nothing could dampen that scream, a shriek ripped viscerally from a body undergoing a level of agony few in history have suffered.

As that cry reached a crescendo, Megrodomigran plucked the throttling skin from the victim's mouth, allowing one bright, clear burst of tormented screeching before he brought his own instrument to bear—a great, scythe-like device.

In an overhanded swipe he split the porter's head, throat and sternum longitudinally, the split extending from the forehead clear to the man's groin.

"Thank the *Sky!*" Ansen burst furiously. "That last blow ended his suffering."

Cries of fright and horror at a fate awaiting them all were audible from the cages up and down the cliff. Surprisingly, Eva and Cecil, like him, were mostly silent and merely observing. Ansen saw that these two were obviously of sterner stuff than he originally believed. He would have expected them both to be shaking like a dog passing razor blades from what they had just seen.

The girl had an eager expression on her face now, while Cecil, who was further away, looked contemplative, almost like a professor observing something in a detached manner upon which he planned one day to write a thesis.

As if that killing blow was a signal to the other natives of this savage isle, they set up a great howl. The sound reminded Ansen of a moaning of supplication, a wailing such as he heard when the women of his tribe prayed over their fallen dead.

Chapter 11: Sacrificed

Originating from below them, those atop the cliffs heard a thunderous grinding as of the parting of earth; it was a deafening roar such as that made by the cataclysmic sliding of seismic plates, the rending of rock and the pouring out of sand from buckets the size of moons. Aghast, Ansen and the others looked from the awful tableau atop the cliff where the porter had been slain, to the foot of the precipice from whence came the sound.

Below them lay a wide, rocky clearing—a preamble to the rocky escarpment over which they hung suspended like bait. From his high seat Ansen saw the jungle begin to blur, and then to pull and spread apart. Deep into the Earth a great rent appeared, a sundering such as might have occurred in the planet's infancy when continental shelves and sea basins were carved with unimaginable and unwitnessed violence.

Ever wider the rent gaped, elongating as well, and deepening, until the molten flow of veins of magma became visible. Ansen watched as the horrid gash assumed a width of over half a mile, twice that in length and so deep that his eyes could not gauge the distance. He dimly guessed he was staring into the Earth's core, a rotating mixture of superheated nickel and iron, but he had an idea that something else drew his eyes, as a hypnotist's pendulum draws the gaze of the mesmerized.

The Blonde Goddess of Tikka-Tikka

At some point the voices of the natives' coalesced in his consciousness—a single, deafening voice made up of hundreds, all chanting the same word, at the same time: Koyltentapharr! Koyltentapharr! Koyltentapharr!

What meant that hideous word? He did not speak their language. Who or what was Koyltentapharr?

Below, the rent in the surface began to darken with a night-black essence that soon clarified into what looked like a nighttime sky, with pinpoints of star light and the gaseous, nebulous smudges of distant galaxies. But nowhere in this "sky" in the rent in the Earth's crust did he see any constellation familiar to him, and he knew them all intimately, having spent a lifetime beneath them.

Out of this other space a monstrous darkness issued forth, nebulously at first, but quickly taking form. Like a giant worm poking its ugly snout out of the ground, it wriggled upward. Its size defied reason, its gaping maw was immense. Circlets of eyes ringed the grotesque body completely around, from which it obviously could see in any and every direction simultaneously.

From the hideous mouth, multiple tongues twisted and snaked, tasting the air of Ansen's world, of which this thing was patently foreign. Far into the air the thing climbed until it looked down upon those gathered upon the cliff. The natives ceased their invocation and Megrodomigran stepped aside, chanting in his unknown speech to this demonic beast he'd summoned from another world—or an alternate reality, Ansen knew not which.

The multiplicity of tongues quickly focused on the porter's body.

"*Attal, Koyltentapharr!*" shouted the wizard of the savages.

The great worm leaned over until its ugly snout hovered just above the body on the blood-soaked altar while its many tongues lapped the spilt gore upon both the altar and the surrounding stone. After a moment the mighty maw spread wide and covered the surface of the stone dais; when it retreated, it left an empty altar. The great beast began to sway as if in ecstasy. It reared its head straight into the air, and Ansen swore he saw its eyes partially close as if it had imbibed the most succulent of viands, while blood dripped and coursed out of the corners of the split that served as its mouth.

Megrodomigran shouted instructions rapidly, as if the need to act quickly was paramount. The men assigned to the task raced to the cliff's edge, selected the next porter in line and pivoted the assembly about until the cage swung over the surface; then they lowered the cage to the rough stone, as before. The whole thing to those who watched was like a nightmare where one cannot escape the horror which chases one through the terror-filled nightscapes of one's mind.

They hauled the next porter from his cage, nearly fainting from his awful, horrific fear, and dragged him toward the stone platform. But as they prepared the next sacrifice the creature, its eyes suddenly slitting with malevolence and intent, moved with blinding speed and gulped one of the porters that was still dangling over the cliff's edge in his cage. Cage and all were consumed at once, the man's pitiable cry cut off succinctly, as if chopped in half by an ax.

Chapter 12: Return of the Ax

Never, thought the Viking, had he endured a more harrowing ordeal than watching the sucking, devouring worm from the abyss go down the line of captives, alternately devouring a man, cage, and all. This explained why some of the cages, his own, in fact, were green and new. At times the summoned entity would pause to enjoy the spectacle of a victim's torture, after which it would devour the corpse lying upon the altar which had by then been reduced to a lifeless, pulpy bag of shattered bones.

After a man lay broken and busted into fragments, the hideous god of these savages would slurp and slaver the corpse with its multiplicity of tongues, finally devouring it, only to wait expectantly for the next torment to begin, reminding Ansen of some hideous dog waiting for its master to toss it a table scrap.

Right down the line of cages came the savages, methodically, ruthlessly—indiscriminately. No man's cries or pleas had any effect upon either the beast or the vile savages who bowed to it. Ansen noted after a while, after many men were tortured and devoured, that the beast had sprouted tentacles from its sides from which more sucking, hungry mouths emerged, each becoming a miniature of its parent, complete with the ring of eyes about each grotesque body.

The man watched in awful fascination as the parent---if such a word can be used for a desecration of nature—lowered its maw to the altar while its newly sprouted young slurped at the split-open, broken, pulverized body, in their exuberance occasionally pulling free limbs to slide down hideous throats.

Ansen glanced down the line at the girl, to Cecil and beyond—a few remaining *askarii* and Wamibi, who was last. The girl seemed mesmerized by the actions of the great worm and its savage worshipers. Her eyes roved avidly as she devoured everything that occurred. She turned her head to Cecil.

"It is time!" she cried.

"Eva!" Ansen shouted. The girl had obviously conceived a plan of escape. "What are you going to do? Eva!"

The girl ignored him as her and Cecil's voices, together, rose in a supplication—a prayer—of their own.

"What in the name of *Father Sky*?" Ansen wondered.

The color of the monster's body had by now deepened to a sullen red, a hideous shade, for all the world as if the blood of its victims coursed through the cells of its body, tinting them with the macabre hue of death. The Norseman had watched in horrified fascination as this process went forward as methodically as a machine, noting the closing gap between himself and his own imminent destruction. His body, hardened by years of privation and a lifetime of adventurous wanderings, tensed like a coil spring, as if he would leap into the clouds the instant his cage was opened.

To all these happenings, the savages responded in exuberant madness, their hide-covered drums and chanting voices pounding out a pulverizing, staccato celebration of their blasphemous, worm-like deity. In gyrations of awful servitude, the tribe danced in geometric patterns, following the path as laid out by the bizarrely spaced torches set in the stone. The sound of the drums and the singsong chanting reminded Ansen of the war drums and dances of his adopted people. But whereas those memories were wholesome and welcome, the things he saw here were not.

With the memories of the past coursing through his mind, he closed his eyes and began chanting the *Ghost Song*—a song which warriors sang before battle. His voice rose and fell with each stanza, his words somehow reverberating over the screams of the tortured and the wails of the island devils, causing disharmony to their chorus.

The worm lunged at one of the remaining *askarii* dangling next to the girl. It occurred so fast Ansen never saw the approach of the beast, as its body lunged past his cage, brushing the girl's enclosure and setting it to swinging wildly over the precipitous fall.

One would think that this would finally produce a squeal of fear from the actress, but it did nothing of the kind. Instead, she laughed! And Cecil chortled as well, joining the girl in some mysterious merriment.

Why did they laugh? Why had the girl not become by now incoherent with fear? Ansen felt that his own courage was at the snapping point. Why was Cecil not comforting her—in his narrow-minded, cowardly way—during her final moments? They continued, chanting in various languages, some of them older than time itself and unknown to him.

Over his own song, Ansen caught a few lines of the girl's prayer spoken in English that became burned in his memory the instant he heard them:

"At Death's dark door, night is born of Light. There, stars are crushed, and galaxies flee in fright. Inside a tempest maelstrom, black spirals careen. Solar winds blow comet dust in a time that's never been. There squats Oth Gokka, Oth Shothok on his right. Mighty gods of chaos—wield thy power and might! Accept this lesser god, its body thy repast. And, too, these mortal clays, that this world might stand aghast!" she cried exuberantly.

But now Ansen's turn had come, and he had no more time to heed these two madmen.

The Blonde Goddess of Tikka-Tikka

His face still raised toward *Father Sky*, Ansen's voice grew firmer and more powerful as he continued to chant the litany of *The People*. If he were home among the great nations his voice would be accompanied by those of the warriors of the tribe, of the village elders—and by the pounding of drums.

The song carried with it the strident strains of war which always bear, as well, the possibility of one's spirit disavowing one's clay. All those who live close to *Mother Earth*, and all those who know *Father Sky*, know that life on the Earth is only a waypoint; that the spirit journey does not end with death, but rather, begins with it.

Ansen was staring into the sky when he felt a tug on his cage. Jerkily, it pivoted about on its rough-hewn, wooden bearing; they brought him around until the bottom of the cage hovered over the solid rock of the cliff at which point they began to lower him. Through it all Ansen's voice never wavered as he sang his death-song. Whatever came, it would not find him lax or wanting.

His strident tones, disrupting the chants of the savages, drew the ire of Megrodomigran, who was obviously the priest as well as the chief of the tribe. He was staring at Ansen as if the Arapaho warrior's song profaned their god. The light of madness and zeal burned in the shaman's eyes. But Ansen only glowered at the chief through the bars and continued his chant undiminished.

Striding over, Megrodomigran shouted words to his men. It appeared the savage wizard wished to put an immediate cessation to Ansen's blasphemy. As they prepared to take him from the cage, Megrodomigran stepped close to the bars, in obvious preparation to thrash the white man about the head and neck.

Having awaited just such an opportunity, the Viking's arm shot through the bars and grasped the chief tightly by his long hair that hung down his blood-smeared breast. With a strength inconceivable the Arapaho warrior jerked the chief from his feet and drew him up against the bars of the roughhewn saplings that comprised Ansen's wooden prison.

Pulled against the cage, the wizard found his face drawn between two of the bars until he hung, his feet off the ground, face-to-face with his intended victim. As he stared into Ansen's eyes he saw no single glimmer of compassion or mercy. He screeched in fear, and his acolytes ran forward. Since Ansen was in the cage they could not attack him and none had their spears; not to mention, this was an offering that must be sacrificed to appease Koyltentapharr, not slaughtered in its cage.

Ansen would have torn at the man's face with his bare teeth, but something else arrested him. In his grappling of the chief he ripped free a priestly robe that the savage was wearing, a badge of his office. As the cape fell from the savage shaman, Ansen glanced down and saw his tomahawk. *Owejiwa* was right there, within his grasp!

He had not seen the ax since the fray in the jungle and had feared it lost to his tribe forever. The thought of losing the talisman, which was precious to his people, had plagued him terribly. For centuries it stood as a token of power to the tribe, bringing them safely through times of strife. He *must* repossess it that it might pass to the next physical manifestation of its spiritual double to whom Owejiwa, the man, must relinquish it, just as had Tahnaktaka.

The weapon protruded from the chief's belt, just within Ansen's reach. The rush of relief he felt might never be conveyed in mere words. With one hand holding the chief, his other shot through the bars and grasped his weapon, which he retrieved and pulled into the cage with him.

"I am Owejiwa!" he shouted.

And in powerful chops, he slammed the tomahawk a half dozen times into the chief's face.

Chapter 13: Food for a God

The wounds were ghastly, cleaving out great, V-shaped chunks of flesh and bone such as an ax might do to an old stump. He released the corpse and, with a single swipe, severed the ropes binding his prison door which he kicked open. He leaped to the top of the cliff where, not for the first time, the savages of this blasphemous isle experienced the war cry of an Arapaho that has just slain a foe.

The great worm seemed unconcerned that its high priest had been killed, and the savages, who'd withdrawn to a safe distance, looked on in horror. Only Megrodomigran's acolytes moved toward Ansen, and these he slaughtered without mercy.

He could still hear the incantations of the two Hollywood elites caged behind him, thinking they had both snapped—their infantile, city-slicker brains shattered by the occurrences of the past day. Cecil's voice came to his ears now that he could focus on something other than slaughtering Megrodomigran and his sub-priests.

"...this sacrifice we have arranged to show our loyalty to thee, O mighty Oth Shothok! O mighty Oth Gokka!"

Before Cecil ceased speaking the air was trembling and vibrating. Ansen stuck his tomahawk into his belt and ran to the cage holding the girl. Her mind may have snapped, but he couldn't leave her to die. The thought of that otherworldly worm devouring her beautiful body was too terrible even for one with Ansen's iron nerves to stomach.

"Eva! I'm going to get you out of this!" he cried. Taking hold of the primitive mechanism, he began turning the immense wooden crane about on its pivot-point by sheer brute force and awkwardness. Slowly, it spun about; lowering her cage became simple now.

When he hacked the rope holding the door fast, he noticed how the girl recoiled from the tomahawk. She had reacted before to the sight of it—while they were aboard the vessel enroute to this awful place. At the time he attributed it to close proximity to a grim weapon of war, representing as it did a wholly gruesome way to die that one so delicate as the Hollywood socialite would obviously find abhorrent.

"Do not fear—this is for those savages," he reassured her, patting the blood-smeared blade absently. He then repeated the exercise to free Cecil. In less than a minute he had the producer's cage lowered to the stone and had cut the door free. Oddly, Cecil, too, recoiled at sight of the bloody weapon.

"Put that away!" he cried.

"Don't be a pantywaist, Cecil. This ax might save your life," Ansen replied brutally, turning back to the girl.

"Behold!" the actress exclaimed, pointing; her gaze held an expression like that of a fanatic.

Looking in the direction indicated, he saw that there was apparently no end in sight to the list of astonishing revelations he must witness this night. He'd dimly wondered why the savages hadn't attacked him while he freed Eva and Cecil; now he understood why.

Across the bloody, sunset sky a tear appeared that spanned the entire firmament. Ansen found the sight so surrealistic that his mouth dropped agape in disbelief. The heavens appeared to have been rent from one pole to the other until the entire sky had been split in twain, separating the east from the west, with planets and cosmoses visible in the cleft unlike any Ansen had seen.

The stars with which he was familiar were gone. The entire sky had split and folded back upon itself, and he was gazing into the secret inner-most recesses of another universe. Then the appearance of the rent changed, and he saw that it wasn't merely a tear but—an immense maw!

"What in the Hell?" Ansen burst. He could not get a distinct sense of the appearance of the entity, but he recognized the tear in the sky to indeed be a cavernous mouth, which meant the creature was immense. But he had only moments to stare before the absurd occurred.

Gravity reversed itself then, with objects falling upward into the sky rather than to the stony ground. The contents of the abyss in the jungle below began falling upward, including the worm-god summoned by Megrodomigran along with that worthy's sycophants, his entire tribe and the shaman's gory corpse.

The savages of Megrodomigran's unknown race stood no chance. He watched them clutch futilely at the bare stone; as well stop a tidal wave with an outstretched hand. One by one they fell, screaming, into the sky where they were consumed by the behemoth jaws.

All were devoured with relish, but special attention was paid to the mastication of the giant worm-god, Koyltentapharr. The clouds of the sky, assuming the shape of immense incisors, gulped the worm of the abyss as one would a special butcher's cut. The wooden mechanisms that supported their prison were the only thing anchored to the stone, and Ansen wasted no time in grabbing hold of one of them just as his feet left the ground.

But the Hollywood socialites, Cecil and Eva, were apparently immune to this bizarre, other-worldly negation of Earth's physics.

The Blonde Goddess of Tikka-Tikka

With the crushing and devouring of the worm-god, gravity returned, and objects began falling from the sky back to the surface. But the chaotic winds that had erupted at the onset of the feeding, when the Earth began falling into this other cosmos, continued to swirl powerfully.

Nearby, Eva muttered her prayers and supplications to this hideous beast in the sky.

Ansen frowned.

This was an affront to *Father Sky*. As powerful as anything he had experienced, he could feel it in the quivering steel of the tomahawk. *Owejiwa* thirsted for the blood of this so-called god with a fierceness that would not be denied!

Chapter 14: Neatly Tricked

Ansen had been played. It wasn't the first time that people had tried to use him. But it was the first time anyone had so utterly succeeded. It made him angry.

Cecil's irritating voice, supplicating the vile creature in the sky, urged it to finish off the remaining porters and *askarii* in their cages even as he groveled and begged to be rewarded for his faithful service. Things weren't falling into the sky any longer, and the winds, although powerful, weren't strong enough to blow him off the cliff, so Ansen let go of the wooden support attached to the stone. He approached the movie producer.

"You lied to me, Cecil," he said.

The girl spun on him. "Did you really think you were worth the price we offered?" she spat.

He eyed her darkly. "So, the movie—all of it—was a sham? An excuse to get everyone here to feed us to that . . . thing," he accused, one finger stabbing toward the rent in the sky. "And here I was starting to like you."

She laughed, shaking her head in disbelief. "You? You, a barbarian, believed the likes of Eva Desyre would—oh, you do flatter yourself, don't you?" she taunted.

"I'm usually confident in my instincts," he replied quietly.

The Blonde Goddess of Tikka-Tikka

He didn't bother looking for Cecil. There was no need. He could tell that the girl was purposely distracting him while the man approached him from a blind side. Without warning he pivoted and faced Cecil who had approached within ten feet of him. In the man's hands was the sickle instrument of Megrodomigran which had fallen to ground where it was then discovered by the movie producer.

"So why me?" he asked the girl over his shoulder without taking his eyes from Cecil.

The girl smiled at his back. "It's all numbers, Ansen Grost. These things are always about the numbers. In our case, we were short—by one. The porters, the *askarii*, we were only missing our leading man—you!" she punctuated with a laugh.

"And here I thought it was my classic good looks and muscular physique," he quipped.

Ansen was stalling until he could figure out how to get himself out of this predicament—and Wamibi, too, who was still in his cage and hopefully alive.

"No," she said, her mocking smile disappearing in an instant. "We had thirty-two; we needed thirty-three."

"I'll admit," Ansen retorted, "that was a slick trick. And I guess I'd have to give you credit for coming up with such an extravagant scheme of offering the god of these savages as a food offering to your own. But sacrificing that worm is one thing. I won't go easily."

Cecil came at him out of nowhere, swinging Megrodomigran's scythe. But the Viking wasn't unarmed; the ancient tomahawk appeared in his hand as if by magic. Ansen ducked Cecil's first swing, then took a sideways swipe at the man's leg. Ansen never knew a foppish weasel like Cecil could move so fast. The producer dodged and riposted with a strike of his own that Ansen barely avoided. But he noticed a look in Cecil's face—the man was staring fixedly at the Norseman's tomahawk, his eyes wide.

"Are you afraid of this, Cecil?" the Viking taunted.

A ghastly look sat frozen on Cecil's face, but he didn't reply. Instead he cast a doubtful glance at the girl, and then ran at Ansen, swinging his weapon and shouting.

"Kill him!" Eva shrieked.

Cecil swung the immense cleaver viciously—desperately. The weapon clanged off the raw stone where Ansen stood a moment before. Ansen rushed him and they clashed. From the onset the Viking had the upper hand. The other man was physically weaker; and although in the right hands his weapon might have been the deadlier with its longer reach, his palpable fear of Ansen's tomahawk crippled his efforts.

Ansen sensed that it wasn't merely a death blow from the weapon that the man feared. Cecil's fear seemed more of an almost supernatural awe of it, which Ansen thought odd for a man who had just summoned an extra-dimensional deity—one of the Old Ones against which the medicine man had warned a young Owejiwa. Cecil couldn't keep his eyes off the ancient ax, but Ansen didn't fool himself into thinking the tomahawk made him invincible.

Without warning something heavy smashed across the Viking's forearm, causing him to drop the tomahawk from an instantly numbed grip.

Cecil came at him hard and fast; Eva had come to her cohort's aid.

"Stupid, filthy barbarian pawn!" she screamed uncontrollably. "Do you think to stop a god? You puny man—your body will be digested in another dimension in the bowel of Oth Shothok, along with that of this woman you care for. Yes—I have seen the desire in your eyes, maggot! Your futile efforts will come to nothing!"

Ansen threw himself into a roll, coming in under the heavy, swinging blade of Megrodomigran. Using his momentum, he launched himself to his feet, throwing a right hook into Cecil's groin that doubled the dandy over and caused him to lose his grip on his chopping sword. Not stopping there, the Norseman followed with a kick and grabbed a staggering Cecil by his shirt front.

Ansen's ham-fist closed up tighter than an oak knot; he rained a number of concussive blows upon the movie producer's face with the force of a hammer man swinging a railroad maul, with each punch carrying the blunt force of a kick from an angry mule. Stunned, Cecil fell to the stone at Ansen's feet.

Glancing about in a sudden panic, Ansen spotted his tomahawk which he dropped when Eva struck him. The girl looked like she wanted to snatch it up to keep it from him, but she dared not touch it. He refused to lose it again. His knotted fist closed upon the brass-studded grip, delighting in the feel of his weapon back in his hand, right where it belonged.

For a moment he felt as Thor must have felt whenever he grasped Mjölnir—a vibrant pulse of energy ran up the corded muscles of his forearm. With grim intent, he stalked toward a dazed Cecil who was struggling to come to his feet.

Not wasting any words, Ansen strode straight up to the Hollywood socialite and slammed the hammer end of the tomahawk into Cecil's temple with all his brute strength, which was considerable. The man's skull burst inward, his eyes bulging from the explosive force. Without any further consideration of the man as a threat, Ansen jerked the bloody weapon from the ruined skull, and Cecil's body hit the stone.

The body began quivering then, as if from some internal goings-ons. The throat bulged, and in a trice a smoky, black object crawled out of the gaping mouth of the corpse. The creature, obviously from the same world as the monstrosities they'd summoned, started to escape but Ansen was too fast for it. In a sideways swing he caught it midways, lopping it in half. Its death throes were disgusting but encouraging.

"At least they can die," he muttered.

Chapter 15: A Token of Power

As if gravity held no sway over the dead creature that ejected itself from Cecil's corpse, its sundered body floated away, hovering about four feet off the ground. Ansen watched as a smoky effluence, pouring from both halves, puddled in the air around the nasty looking carcass—the vapory ichor of the abomination.

Horrified, the girl went from gloating to shrieking in terror as she fled from Ansen Grost and his tomahawk. He ran her down, grasping her by her long, blonde locks. She squealed in otherworldly fright when he jerked her off her feet to fall on the hard, stone surface of the cliff. She rolled over and stared in horror at the frightening tomahawk and then her eyes rolled back into her head and the girl's body began convulsing.

"*Holy Sky!*" Ansen burst, recoiling in repugnance.

As had occurred with Cecil, a creature—not really solid and definitely not of this world—crawled out from the beautiful girl. As the thing fled into the sky away from Ansen and his ax the girl's head lolled sideways; she was unconsciousness.

"What are these things?" Ansen muttered in disgust. Then he noted the rapid movement of shadows slithering across the stone of the precipice.

The Blonde Goddess of Tikka-Tikka

He had momentarily forgotten the rent sky and the amorphous beings summoned by Cecil and Eva. He jerked his face skyward in time to see an immense mouth descending toward the top of the cliff—toward him! Pouring out of it were countless numbers of the small, dark things like those that had abandoned the bodies of the Hollywood socialites, circling him like vultures awaiting their prey to become too helpless to prevent their feeding upon him.

He had only a moment to react and did so with an instinct that had guided many others that the talisman had chosen to bear it across the surface of the physical world over the centuries.

Ansen could not know it, but the tomahawk was only the token's latest form, having taken a shape that the Arapaho admired and revered. In other times, it had been a sword, a war hammer, a shield—whatever form it needed to take that it might fulfill its destiny.

Ansen, he heard a voice speak.

For one, still moment, time paused.

"I am here," he said aloud.

Slay, the voice commanded.

Ansen's great fist gripped the studded handle of the ax while his storm-colored eyes stared venom at the descending monstrosity of another time or dimension, he knew not which. The man's entire body tensed like a tightly wound spring and then, in a burst of pure, raw power, his arm—drawn back to a position far behind his head—shot forward and released the tomahawk.

The ax spun, end over end, straight into the descending maw which, due to its proximity, he could in no way miss. The beast of cosmic chaos had no chance to dodge the flying missile. The tear in the sky screamed, and began curling, inside out. The torn edges of the sky started coming back together, closing the tear in the firmament and hiding the death throes of the pair of outer cosmic deities.

With a force that might have blasted an anvil into atoms, the tomahawk flashed out of the closing rift as the tear closed, twirling end over end to slam, blade-first, into the altar and shattering it. The disembodied creatures of smoky darkness, along with the abnormal beast that had vacated the girl's body, fled into the sky where they were sucked into the closing rent as the whole thing collapsed.

Above Ansen's head was now an innocuous, sunset-colored sky with recognizable stars already reappearing.

At the foot of the cliff the gaping abyss was gone, having closed with the death of Koyltentapharr, the worm god worshipped by the people of this mysterious isle. The savages themselves were gone, every last one of them eagerly devoured by Oth Gokka and Oth Shothok—the bizarre deities of a dimensional aberration that split the heavens, creating a door from Ansen's world to theirs that they might feed on mortals and lesser gods— only to discover their own mortality, thanks to Ansen and his ax.

Leaving the girl where she lay for the time being, Ansen went to Wamibi and pivoted the headman's cage about on its fulcrum.

"Great *bwana*! You live!" the black man exclaimed.

Ansen smiled. It was typical of Wamibi to delight in Ansen's welfare with no consideration to his own. He was a good man, and a faithful friend.

"Yes, Wamibi! And you, too, thank the *Sky*," he replied.

Having released the headman of the *askarii*, of which not a soul survived, they approached the girl who, still dazed, was now sitting up. Ansen helped her to her feet and steadied her.

The Blonde Goddess of Tikka-Tikka

"Are you alright, Miss Desyre?" he asked, unsure if it was actually the girl, or some otherworldly entity, who might answer him.

"Wh-what happened? Where am I?" she asked; her expression was one of confoundment.

"What do you remember?" he asked her gently.

"The last thing I recall is being at the studio. I was in my dressing room, rehearsing lines and dressing for a shot. There was a knock. I—I can't seem to recall anything after that…" she trailed off.

"My name is Ansen—Ansen Grost. And this is Wamibi. Come, Miss Desyre, we have a long journey back to Zanzibar. We'll fill you in on the way," he said.

"Please, Mr. Grost, you're too kind—call me Eva," she said, smiling. "Did you say Zanzibar?"

Ansen strode over to the former altar of the savages and retrieved his tomahawk, marveling that the ax had not splintered into fragments. The solid stone altar was nothing but rubble, but the talisman of the Arapaho stood firm, although it looked perhaps a bit more scarred to the Viking's eyes.

As he retrieved it, it made a grating sound sliding free of the stone, reminding him of the Arthurian legends of yore. His brows contracted as he looked hard at the ax, wonderingly. Could it be? Shaking his head, he slid the weapon in his belt, and returned to his friends.

After leaving the cliffs, the trio hiked to the beach upon which they had landed days earlier. With relief, they found their ship floating offshore, unharmed. The captain and crew were delighted to see Ansen, Wamibi and Eva, and lamented the loss of the porters and Wamibi's boys. As to Cecil's fate, they could care less; he had treated them like sub-humans.

Himself a wanderer, Ansen invited the girl to join him on his journey to visit the land of his parents where he was determined to visit, after which he would escort her to America. He had never gone home after the war and his heart yearned to visit the medicine man who raised him. It was time to return to *The People* . . . if only for a season or so.

Strangely drawn to the man, she agreed.

The End

Consummatum est

An Invitation…

Dear reader,

I hope you enjoyed this tale. I wish to extend an invitation to leave feedback for this story in the form of a review should you be so inclined.

And if you liked this story you might be interested in my other works, specifically Tales of the Tomahawk Volume II, *The Banshee of the Atacama.*

Consider visiting my site for descriptions of other stories that might appeal to you. I'm always working to add to my published library, so check back from time to time. And thanks.

www.ChrisLAdamsBizareTales.com

Best regards,

Chris

The Banshee of the Atacama

Volume II of the series, Tales of the Tomahawk

In the aftermath of a dust-up in the pub where he is staying, Ansen is befriended by an old man who—once he sees the Norseman fight—offers him an interesting job.

To make it hard to refuse, the pay is better than just right. Down-on-his-luck Ansen can hardly refuse. After all, a guy has to earn a living . . . and fighting cosmic entities and supernatural bad guys doesn't put ale in a glass or food in a belly.

But this job involves finding a Scottish lass lost in Peru. And she's not like other girls. This lass has a centuries-old banshee as a familiar who can be slightly over-protective.

This might get hairy.

Acknowledgements

I wish to extend my heartfelt gratitude to my wife who listens as I go on and on about my stories. I know she must sometimes tire of hearing about plots and characters, but she always listens. Thanks, honey.

I wish to express my gratitude to my friend, Scott, with whom I share many common interests. As such, we frequently talk about stories. He has helped me out of several writing conundrums, offering his sage advice along the way.

After reading their stories for years I must acknowledge the fine authors who influenced me from beyond (for many of them have sailed the Darkling Sea, as McKiernan would say) to give something back to the rich world of well-spun tales I've enjoyed since I was a youth.

I also thank God for giving me whatever it is that drives me to write stories. I just have one favor to ask: keep 'em coming!

About the Author

Chris spent years playing guitar in and out of bands and was, during that time, more of a voracious reader than a writer. After that last band collapsed, he turned from writing songs to writing stories, eventually turning out a six-volume Barsoom series as a tribute to Edgar Rice Burroughs (currently under contract to Edgar Rice Burroughs Inc.) and several self-published short stories and poems.

Chris has a creative side, and so together with writing and playing guitar, he also dabbles in painting (the covers for *The Hunter and the Sorcerer* and *A Savage from Atlantis* are his).

You may find him on his website where you'll find links and information on available stories, and other things you might find of interest (be sure to check out the Fantasy Art page.)

Chris enjoys discussing favorite authors, writing and collecting books so feel free to shoot him an email from his Contact page.

Chris resides in Southern West Virginia with his wife and two children.

www.ChrisLAdamsBizarreTales.com

Time Frames of Ansen's Life

1893   Born to Hanlo and Elisabet Grost

1896   Parents slain. Ansen captured — age 3

1897   Adopted by Tahnaktaka — age 4

1914   Leaves the Arapaho to join the US Army — age 21

1917   USA declares war, departs for France — age 24

1918   Discharged from US Army — age 25

'18-'24   Globetrotting — age 25-31

1925   *The Blonde Goddess of Tikka-Tikka* — age 32

1926   *The Banshee of the Atacama* — age 33

Bizarre Tales

Bizarre Tales © is the colophon under which Chris writes and publishes stories.

To keep up with what Chris is working on, check out the Bizarre Tales Blog on GoodReads:

https://www.goodreads.com/author/show/15259542.Chris_L_Adams/blog

And be sure to visit the official Bizarre Tales © website at www.ChrisLAdamsBizarreTales.com.

Look for the BT logo on the cover!

List of Works

Currently available:

- The Valley of Despair (Tales of Despair 1)
- The Cosmos of Despair (Tales of Despair 2)
- On A Winter's Eve
- The Treasure of Akram el-Amin
- The Blonde Goddess of Tikka-Tikka (Tales of the Tomahawk 1)
- The Banshee of the Atacama (Tales of the Tomahawk 2)
- Atlas of the Serpent Men (A Tale of Conan of Cimmeria)
- Conan and Old Crem (A Tale of Conan of Cimmeria)
- The Hunter and the Sorcerer (Prehistoric Tales 1)
- A Savage from Atlantis (Prehistoric Tales 2)
- Dark Tides of Mars (A Tale of Barsoom 1) – Published by Edgar Rice Burroughs Inc.

Coming next:

- Gauntlets of Mars (A Tale of Barsoom 2) – Published by Edgar Rice Burroughs Inc.
- Untitled (Tales of the Tomahawk 3)
- Untitled (Prehistoric Tales 3)

www.ingramcontent.com/pod-product-compliance
Lightning Source LLC
Chambersburg PA
CBHW051926220626
47052CB00003B/592